KISHKA for KOPPEL

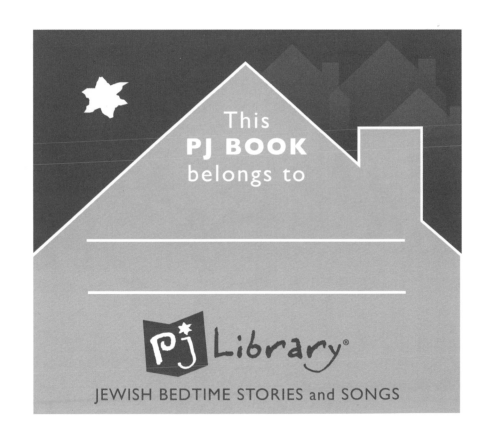

This **PJ BOOK** belongs to

_____

_____

The junk jiggled in Koppel's cart as he pushed it down the dusty lane. His shoulders hurt and his back ached. His legs felt heavy, like Mama's noodle pudding.

Koppel stopped beside a big trash can and looked in. He pulled out a moldy sock, a cracked cup and a torn rubber boot. Then he spotted an old iron meat grinder with a wooden handle.

"Just another piece of rusty junk," he said. **"Why am I so unlucky?"**

Koppel tossed the meat grinder into his cart.

"Unlucky?" said a voice. "If you sell umbrellas and it never rains, that's unlucky."

Koppel turned around. No one was there. **"Who's talking? Where are you?"**

"Sure your father was a great rabbi and you're a junkman," said the voice, "but unlucky you're not."

The peddler eyeballed the meat grinder. He picked it up, turned it over and gave it a shake.

"Take it easy, Koppel. I may be a meat grinder, but I've got feelings."

Koppel's mouth dropped open. "A talking meat grinder," he said. "How do you know my name? How do you know my father was a rabbi?"

"My lips are sealed."

"You don't have any lips."

"Never mind, I'm here to help you."

Koppel scratched his head. "Are you the prophet Elijah? He helps people too."

"Do I look like Elijah? Be quiet already and listen." The grinder twirled its crank. "I'll give you three wishes. You can have anything you want. Just make a wish and turn my crank."

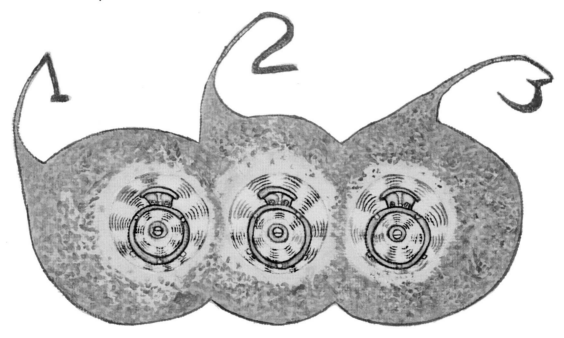

"I don't believe in magic wishes." Koppel sniffed.

"And I suppose you don't believe in talking meat grinders?"

Koppel laughed. "You're a sharp cookie for a meat grinder."

He chucked it back into the cart and raced home to his wife.

"Yetta! Yetta! Good news!" shouted Koppel.

Yetta put her hands on her hips. "Finally business is good! You can take me to the movies maybe?"

"No, this is better than money." Koppel grinned. "We have three wishes. We can wish for anything."

"What are you talking about?"

Koppel plunked the meat grinder down on the table. "Tell her what you told me," he said.

Yetta rolled her eyes. "Oy vey, he's talking to a meat grinder."

"Tell her!" shouted Koppel.

The meat grinder was silent.

"Does it know any chicken jokes?" Yetta giggled. "It sings 'My Yiddishe Mama' maybe?"

Yetta laughed so hard she popped three buttons. But Koppel didn't notice.

He had a faraway look in his eyes.

"Imagine, Yetta. If you really had three wishes, for what would you wish?"

"I wish you would fix the leaky tap," said Yetta. "And the walls could use some paint too."

Koppel frowned. "Yetta, please try."

"All right, already," she said.

Yetta's eyes grew soft and dreamy.

"I'd wish for a pearl necklace and earrings to match."

Koppel laughed. "I'd wish for the whole jewelry store."

"I'd wish to be young and beautiful." She sighed.

"I'd wish I was a prince. Then I'd take you to the royal ball."

"I'd wish I was a queen in a golden palace on a mountain of cheesecake with cherries."

With each wish, their eyes gleamed brighter.

His Royal Koppelness

Koppel chuckled. "This wishing makes me hungry like a horse. My bubby made a kishka the King of China would eat," he said. "I wish I had a piece this big."

Koppel flung his arms wide and bumped the meat grinder's crank. It spun around with a terrible screech. A huge hunk of steaming kishka flopped onto a plate.

"Oops," said Koppel.

Yetta's face turned red like beets.

"YOU HAD ANY WISH IN THE WORLD, AND YOU WISHED FOR STUFFED SHEEP GUTS?"

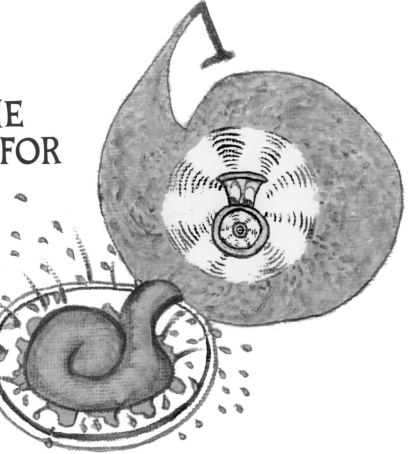

Koppel winced. "I made a little mistake."

Yetta's eyes bulged like turnips. "A little mistake? I'll show you a mistake!

I WISH THIS KISHKA WOULD STICK TO YOUR NOSE!"

Yetta grabbed the crank and spun it with all her might. The kishka leapt in the air and glued itself to Koppel's nose. It dangled down to his belly button.

"Yetta! What have you done?"

Yetta clapped her hands to her face. "I went a little cuckoo. I'm sorry."

Koppel grabbed the kishka and pulled. It wouldn't budge. "Help!" he said.

Yetta yanked it as hard as she could. She tugged and tugged.

"Stop! You're pulling my nose off!"

She let go, and Koppel tumbled to the floor.

"It's stuck," she panted. "It won't come off."

"Now we have only one wish left," he groaned.

"We should wish for the golden palace," said Yetta.

"What about this kishka on my nose?"

"I think you look very distinguished, Koppel."

"I look like an elephant!"

"You can join the circus maybe? At last you can make some big money."

Tears and kishka juice dribbled onto Koppel's pants.

Yetta suddenly felt very sorry for her husband. "Koppel, I wish the kishka would drop from your nose."

She gave the crank a good spin. The kishka plopped back on the plate.

With joyful tears, Koppel waltzed his wife around the room.

"Thank you, Yetta! Thank you so much!"

But Yetta looked glum. Koppel stopped dancing.

"I guess we're still as poor as ever." He sighed.

Suddenly, the grinder cranked its crank.

"Oy, he's still complaining! Koppel, stop and think. Look a little closer."

Koppel peered out the window and all around the house. He stared at the kishka and looked at his wife. Then he burst out laughing. "He has no head, Yettela, but the grinder talks sense."

"What do you mean?" she asked.

Koppel's eyes sparkled as he took Yetta's hands. "A loving wife. A little kishka. Who could wish for more?"

Yetta kissed her Koppel on the nose. "Some tea with your kishka, Koppela?"

GLOSSARY

Bubby—the Yiddish word for "grandmother"

Elijah—a Hebrew prophet of the ninth century BC, who championed the worship of God (I Kings 17–21:21; II Kings 1–2:18); in Jewish folklore, he travels the world in disguise, trying to help humanity

kishka (kishke)—an Eastern European meat often eaten by Jews; it is a boiled and slowly roasted cow or sheep intestine stuffed with flour, chicken fat and spices, and served with gravy

Koppel—a Yiddish pet name for the Hebrew Yaaqob or Jacob, meaning "head" or "deep thinker"

"My Yiddishe Mama" (My Yiddishe Momme)—a song written by Jack Yellen and Lew Pollack, made famous by singer Sophie Tucker in 1925, after the death of her mother

noodle pudding—a non-dairy European Jewish dish, often made with apples and raisins; cooked for the Sabbath and other Jewish holidays

Oy vey—"Oh no!" or "Woe is me!"

rabbi—a learned, authoritative teacher of Jewish law, ritual and tradition; commonly trained and ordained to lead a Jewish congregation or synagogue

Yetta—a Polish-Jewish pet name for Henrieta, meaning "mistress of the house"

Library and Archives Canada Cataloguing in Publication

Davis, Aubrey
Kishka for Koppel / Aubrey Davis; illustrated by Sheldon Cohen.

Issued in print and electronic formats.
ISBN 978-1-55469-299-6 (bound).— ISBN 978-1-4598-0073-1 (pbk.).—
ISBN 978-1-5546-9300-9 (pdf).— ISBN 978-1-4598-0622-1 (epub)

I. Cohen, Sheldon, 1949– II. Title.
PS8557.A832K58 2011   jc813'.54   C2011-903503-0

First published in the United States, 2011
Library of Congress Control Number: 2011929241

Summary: A magic meat grinder helps a poor Jewish couple learn a little gratitude after the three wishes it grants them go awry.

Orca Book Publishers is dedicated to preserving the environment and has printed this book on Forest Stewardship Council® certified paper.

Orca Book Publishers gratefully acknowledges the support for its publishing programs provided by the following agencies: the Government of Canada, the Canada Council for the Arts and the Province of British Columbia through the BC Arts Council and the Book Publishing Tax Credit.

Cover and interior artwork created using acrylic paints on canvas board.

Cover artwork by Sheldon Cohen
Design by Teresa Bubela

ORCA BOOK PUBLISHERS
orcabook.com

Printed and bound in Canada.

22 21 20 19 • 5 4 3 2

061929.5K2/B388/A8